MAXIMUS AND THE GREAT EXPEDITION

Contents

Maximus hibernates   5
Don't miss out by being lazy

The great expedition   10
Friends help us do things

Some are different   15
God made us all different

Tooth drill   20
It's important to keep healthy

Happy Christmas   25
Jesus is the best Christmas present

Why be bored?   30
Using time well

Saints alight!   35
Making the world a happier place

A load of rubbish   40
Caring for the world around us

You are who you are   45
Making the best of ourselves

What a wonderful world   50
Appreciating the world God made

When in doubt, read the instructions   55
The Bible

Good for something   60
Using our gifts

Maximus and the great expedition

One of the things that children ask Maximus and me as we visit schools is how do we write the stories. I explain that we start with a theme – something which might be a worry, like bullying or being brave, or going to the dentist. Often these themes are suggested by children when we discuss the stories. We would like to thank all those children, and some adults, who have helped us with this book.

Maximus hasn't changed much from the earlier happenings. He still manages to get into trouble just as often but he has several very good friends like Patrick and Paula who are usually there to rescue him.

We would like to thank all those very kind people who have taken the trouble to write to us and send us lovely pictures of Maximus. We hope you will enjoy these stories, whether you read them at home, or hear them in Assembly.

Maximus and I would especially like to thank Elke for all the really great illustrations once again.

We dedicate this book to Eleanor and hope that she will enjoy these stories when she is a little older.

Maximus Mouse and Brian Ogden

MAXIMUS

and the
Great Expedition

Brian Ogden
Illustrated by Elke Counsell

Scripture Union

By the same author
Maximus Mouse
Maximus Rides Again
Maximus and the Computer Mouse
Short Tails and Tall Stories

Maximus books in colour
Maximus and the Lettuce Thieves
Maximus has a Bad Day
Maximus and The Television
Maximus goes on Holiday

© Brian Ogden 1995
First published 1995
Reprinted 1997, 1999

Scripture Union, 207–209 Queensway,
Bletchley, Milton Keynes, MK2 2EB

ISBN 0 86201 939 7

British Library Cataloguing-in-Publication Data
A catalogue record for this book is available from the British
Library.

Phototypeset by Input, London
Printed and bound in Great Britain by Cox and Wyman Ltd,
Reading.

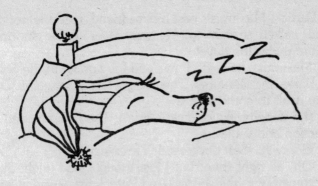

Maximus hibernates

It was very quiet in the vestry. Outside the birds were singing, the wind was whistling because he was happy, and the sun was playing hide and seek behind several large grey clouds. Inside it seemed as though nothing was moving. In fact unless you got very close to the tiny tissue duvet in one corner you might think that there was no living creature in the vestry. But if you were to lay the tip of your finger, very gently, on the duvet you would feel an up and down sort of movement. The sort that means that there might just be some small creature breathing slowly. The creature was a mouse – a mouse named Maximus, who lived in the vestry of St. Michael's Church.

If you had walked through the church towards the vestry you might have seen a small scrap of paper pinned to the bottom of the door. If you had bent right down low you would have read these words:

I HAM IBIN8ING
sined
MAXIMUS
PS DO KNOT DISTUB

Patrick, Maximus's best mouse friend, read the notice and walked straight in. He went over to the snoring figure under the duvet.

'Maximus,' he said, 'Paula and I are going to the Sale in Barks and Dentures. They've got lots of bargains. Do you want to come with us?'

The sleeping figure gave a grunt. The duvet moved a fraction and spoke.

'Go away. Can't you read? I'm asleep.'

'Oh, all right then, but I just thought you might like to come out to the shops.' And Patrick tip-pawed away, back to his family.

Half an hour later there was the sound of flapping wings in the church. It was Barnabas, the church bat, who lived in the belfry. He swooped low, straight through the door, and landed upside down, clinging to the vicar's coathanger.

'Maximus, my dormant rodent companion, I am visiting an emporium of great educational expectation this very day – namely the Battish Museum. I would consider it both a pleasure and an honour should you accompany me on this academic expedition.'

The figure under the duvet poked a nose and whiskers outside the duvet and grunted again. The whiskers twitched and there was a loud sneeze.

'Go away. Can't you read? I'm asleep.'

'Oh, very well. What a Philistine you are. Education is obviously wasted on mice,' said Barnabas and flew away, disturbing the dust once more. Another sneeze followed the first and the duvet lay still.

At the time when Maximus would usually be chasing around looking for something to eat for lunch, another visitor appeared. It was a very prickly ball with little black feet and a small black snout. The prickly ball was called Herbert, one of the hedgehogs who lived in the churchyard.

'Maximus, dear old friend, I come with an invitation,'

said the old hedgehog. 'We are having a birthday party today for my granddaughter Hyacinth. Her mother, my daughter Henrietta, has cooked all sorts of delicious delicacies – there's ant custard, earthworm spaghetti and rotten apple pie. Do please come. All the family would love to see you.'

There was a slight movement under the duvet and, had the old hedgehog's hearing been better, he would have recognised the smacking of mousey lips.

'Go away. Can't you read? I'm asleep,' said the duvet.

A little later, about after school time, a furry figure bounced into the vestry and over to the duvet. It had large stuck up ears and a sort of ball of cotton wool at the back. It was Robin, the youngest son of Robert and Roberta, all of whom lived in a burrow in the churchyard.

'Maximus, old buddy,' said Robin, 'just where are you at? We had a date with a football. We need you between the posts. Come on Max – like now.' The duvet shivered. No more than the tip of a whiskered nose poked out.

'Go away. Can't you read? I'm asleep.'

The rabbit hopped off to play.

Round about the time when the sun rested his head on a large cloud and went to sleep, the duvet moved. First, it went up in the air like a tent, and then it fell again like a burst balloon. Maximus appeared from under the duvet and stretched his front legs, and then his back legs. He yawned and spoke to the empty vestry.

'It must be the spring. Time for hibernating animals to get up and to eat.' He walked into the church. Coming from the Sunday School cupboard was the most whisker twitching, nose grabbing smell. It was more than a smell. It was pure delight. 'That's . . . er, hymnburgers with candle sauce and are there some . . .? Er, yes definitely, sermon note chips,' said Maximus to the empty church. He knocked on the door.

'Oh, woken up, have we?' said Paula. 'Don't tell me, I know, you've sniffed supper. Come on in then.'

'I've been hibernating,' said Maximus.

'Rubbish,' said Patrick. 'You've been lazy. You've stayed in bed doing nothing but sleeping. Well, you missed lots of bargains at Barks and Dentures and, from what I have heard, a very good party for Hyacinth.'

'Barnabas told me he had a really interesting day at the Battish Museum,' added Paula, 'and Robin was saying something about how they had found a really good new goalkeeper for their football team.'

'Oh dear,' said Maximus, 'perhaps hibernating isn't a good thing for mice?'

'Being lazy isn't a good thing for mice,' said Patrick and Paula together.

Heavenly Father,
It's very easy to spend our time doing nothing. Teach us that we miss out on so much by being lazy. Help us to do the best both for ourselves and for others and to use time sensibly. Amen.

The great expedition

Maximus and Patrick had decided it the night before. The next day they would explore parts of the church which other mice had not reached. They would take food in case they needed a snack, strong boots would be worn, and old jeans as some of the church was a bit dusty. They would meet at eight o'clock outside the vestry door.

As the church clock began to get all excited about its eight o'clock strike, making great whirring noises, two small furry creatures greeted each other. One had a long piece of string over its shoulder – the other had a knapsack.

'This is the moment,' said Maximus grandly. 'This day shall go down in the history books. "The Great Explanation of St Michael's Church" will long be remembered.'

'Maximus, it's actually Exploration not Explanation,' Patrick corrected him.

'Well, whatever it is, we are going to do it. Right then Patrick, best paws forward.'

'Excuse me, Maximus, but where are we going? I

mean, in which direction?' asked Patrick.

'I have been thinking about this,' said Maximus. 'Humans have been to the North Pole and to the South Pole. We shall be the first mice to reach the Flag Pole!'

The two brave mice moved slowly through the church singing songs of exploration.

> *Nothing shall us defeat,*
> *We shall conquer all,*
> *Our journey we'll complete,*
> *Even though we're small.*

After nearly ten minutes they reached the door of the church tower. There was room to squeeze under the door as the step had become very worn over the years. They started to climb.

'Porridge, Patrick,' panted Maximus. 'We shall succeed.'

'Courage, Maximus – courage, not porridge,' replied his friend as they continued the climb. After a short while they began to feel a draught. At first it was very gentle but as they got higher it became quite a strong wind.

'All explorers face bad weather,' said Maximus as they stopped for a break. 'Spot of the Antarctic battled against dreadful winds. I remember hearing about him at school.'

'Well, I think we're nearly at the bell chamber. Perhaps Barnabas will be up and about,' said Patrick.

They struggled on nobly against the breeze and soon toppled over the last step into the bell chamber. It seemed very bright after the darkness of the stairway up. They blinked against the light and then saw what looked like a pair of leather gloves hanging upside down from a bell rope, tied to the wall. It was Barnabas the bat.

'I must be hallucinating,' exclaimed Barnabas. 'I thought I saw two mice.'

'You aren't and you did,' said Maximus. 'Well, that is,

I don't think you are, but I know we is.'

'How quite extraordinary. Two examples of Mus Musculus in my domain. A rare occurrence in the chronicles of my campanile. I suppose you require my superior intelligence to unravel some minuscule problem?'

'No thank you, Barnabas,' replied Patrick, 'not on this occasion. We are merely passing through to higher things!'

'Yes,' added Maximus, 'we're going to discover the Flag Pole.'

Barnabas looked a little surprised but promptly went back to sleep. Then, as the mice crept quietly over the floor towards a ladder, he opened one eye and spoke.

'Just travel silently and do not expect me to rescue you from your inept attempts at exploration.'

The two brave mice climbed slowly up the ladder towards the wooden ceiling above them.

'Er, . . . Patrick, I'm not very good at heights,' whispered Maximus.

'Just don't look down. Keep looking at the next step above you.'

Soon they had reached the next floor and could see all the bells gleaming in the sunshine which slid in between the slatted windows.

'Aren't they big!' said Maximus.

'I hope they don't suddenly ring,' said Patrick.

'Where do we go now?' asked Patrick.

'Home would be a good idea,' muttered Maximus. 'Well, to reach the Flag Pole we need to get out on the roof. We shall have to climb again. 'Er . . . you wouldn't like me to stay here and guard the knapsack, would you? It's very high and I'm feeling . . .'

'No, Maximus,' said Patrick, 'in the words of the Three Mouseketeers, "All for one, and one for all". We go on together, in other words.'

They struggled up yet another ladder, passing the shining bells, and out onto the flat roof of the church

tower. There in front of them was the end of their journey. What they had set out to reach nearly an hour and a half ago. What no mouse had ever reached – the Flag Pole!

'We've done it! We're here where no mouse has treadded before,' said Maximus, overcome by the occasion.

'You've done really well, Maximus,' said Patrick. 'I know how much you hate heights, yet you've come all the way up here. I think you're very brave.'

'I was very frightened by all the climbing,' said Maximus. He was talking the next day to Patrick and Paula's children. 'But your dad kept me going. He's a real friend. He made me believe that I could do it. But not without him.'

And all the children cheered the two brave mice.

Heavenly Father,
There are times in our lives when we have to be brave. Help us to remember that Jesus is the friend who is always near us and with his help we can overcome fear. Amen.

Some are different

'Ready?' whispered Maximus.

'Right,' said Patrick.

'Now!' ordered Maximus.

There was the most frightening noise. The two mice rattled tins with pebbles in them, Maximus shouted and screamed at the top of his voice and Patrick blew a toy trumpet. After a few moments, just as Maximus decided he couldn't carry on any longer, a head appeared on the tree above them. It was a roundish head with large staring eyes and it looked rather cross.

'I have had mice like you for supper,' said the head. 'Go away now or I might have an early breakfast.'

The two mice turned and scampered off through the long grass. After a while they stopped, rather out of breath.

'That really woke him up,' panted Maximus. 'What a great laugh! No animal should sleep during the day – it's not natural.'

'I didn't like the look in his eyes,' said Patrick. 'I don't really fancy being owl breakfast. I hope Mr Toot forgets what we did.'

Earlier, the two mice had been talking about some of the other animals who lived near St Michael's Church.

'Rabbits, rats, voles, squirrels, all the creepy crawly bugs and of course mice, sleep at night,' said Maximus. 'It's the only sensible thing to do. Can you imagine any well brought up mouse wandering around in the dark? It would bump into things. It's just not natural to sleep during the day. I, er . . . that is *we*, must do something about it.'

'What sort of thing did you have in mind?' asked his worried friend, Patrick.

'Education!' replied Maximus grandly. 'A bit of education. Er . . . we must teach these animals where they go wrong. We must show them how much more sensible it would be to sleep at night and be awake during the day.'

'They might not like it,' argued Patrick. 'They may say they are happy as they are.'

'Doesn't matter,' said Maximus. 'We know they are wrong. One day they will thank us – all the owls and bats and hedgehogs. They will learn that it is easier to see in the light and sleep in the dark. Let's start with Mr Toot.'

'Maximus, old friend, is that really a good idea? I mean, Mr Toot does rather fancy mice pudding. I'm not keen on being on his menu.'

'Porridge, Patrick – er, sorry, that should be 'courage', Patrick. Mr Toot shall be the first. We'll make a loud noise under his tree and wake him up and then he will see what it's like in the day and then he will thank us and say what clever mice we are,' said Maximus, rather out of breath.

Patrick was not at all sure that his friend was right. Perhaps there were some creatures who were supposed to be up during the night and down during the day. Perhaps they wouldn't like being told they were wrong.

'But what if we're wrong?' asked Patrick. 'What if

animals should sleep during the day and be out at night?'

'Patrick, don't be silly. My great uncle Shakepaw used to say "Day to reap, Night to sleep". There is no doubt about it.'

Maximus and Patrick scampered back to the vestry after their hard work waking up Mr Toot.

'That was a good start,' said Maximus. 'Now, we must think who's going to be next. I reckon we should try Herbert.'

Herbert was the hedgehog who lived in the church-yard and who sniffled around during the night looking for slugs and worms to eat.

'He's got to be here somewhere,' said Maximus.

'I think I heard him over there,' said Patrick pointing towards a large gravestone.

'Well, let's try. . . . aaaaaah,' yelled Maximus.

'Maximus, are you all right? In fact are you . . . er, I mean, where are you?'

Maximus had disappeared. He had fallen into a deep and very wet hole and was paddling around and trying to shout at the same time. It was getting dark and Patrick could not see. He decided to go back to the vestry for a candle. On his way he stumbled over what he thought was a piles of leaves. There was a snuffling sound and then a shape slowly pushed its way out and said,

'You know, I don't think it's sensible for you day-time animals to be out after dark – you might get lost.' It was Herbert!

It took Herbert and his family most of the night to rescue Maximus, who was very cold and very muddy and very sorry.

'I've . . . er . . . been doing some thinking,' said Maximus when he met Patrick after breakfast. 'I could just be wrong about night and day. Perhaps some animals are supposed to be awake at night and others during the day.'

'I'm sure they are,' replied his friend, 'and that doesn't make them wrong. It just makes them different from us.'

Heavenly Father,
You made many kinds of people, some are black and some are white, some do things in different ways from us. Help us to understand that we are all your people and help us to live together in love. Amen.

Tooth drill

'I think it was that sermon note chop that did it,' said Paula. 'You really had to chew it over properly.'

'All I know is . . . ouch!' squealed Maximus, holding his front paw to his mouth, 'I've got terrible tooth-ache.'

'Dentist for you, Maximus. You must go and see Mr Pullem. He'll sort out your bad teeth.'

'I don't like dentists – they do nasty things.'

'When did you go last, Maximus?' asked Paula. 'It sounds like rather a long time ago.'

'Well, let me see,' said Maximus. 'I think it was just before you and Patrick came to live in the church. I remember I had a bad tooth after the Harvest Festival.'

'That is ages ago,' said Paula. 'No wonder your teeth are hurting. You need to go every six months – not every six years! I shall make an appointment for you when I go shopping later this morning.'

'Oh please don't. I'm sure it will be better by then,' begged Maximus. But Paula wouldn't listen to him and an appointment was made for that afternoon.

Maximus walked very slowly out of the church. Already he was sure that this tooth was feeling a lot better. Funny how that happens when you are actually going to the dentist. He crossed the road and went slowly down the High Street passing shops like Barks and Dentures, Mousco and Bootees. Outside the dentist was a shining brass plate which read *I. Pullem – Qualified Dentist*. Maximus pushed open the door and was asked to sit in the waiting room. There were three young squirrels being told to keep quiet by their mother, an old and nearly toothless hedgehog, and Robert the rabbit.

'Hi, Maximus,' said Robert. 'Come to see old Pullem, have you?'

Maximus groaned. He didn't feel like talking to anyone he knew – least of all being cheerful about it.

'Well, I've had a bit of toothache but it's better now so I think I won't waste the dentist's time. He's going to be busy with this lot. Bye, Robert.'

Maximus stood up and walked to the door. He hoped the receptionist would be busy as he tip-pawed past her window. He was just pushing the front door open when she spoke.

'Excuse me, Mr Maximus, but is there something wrong? Mr Pullem won't be long. You're next to see him.'

'That's what I'm afraid of,' whispered Maximus to himself. 'No, it's just that the ache has gone,' he said aloud, 'and I don't want to waste Mr Pullem's time.'

'I'm sure that he will want to find out what made the tooth ache.' At that moment a voice came out of the loudspeaker.

'Mr Maximus, please. Mr Pullem will see you now.'

Maximus was caught. He couldn't escape without the other patients and the receptionist seeing him and the dentist was ready. He turned round and walked very slowly to the door marked *Mr I. Pullem*.

'Good afternoon, Mr Maximus. How can I help you? It's a long time since you were here.'

'Well, er . . . I've had a little bit of toothache but . . . er . . . it's better now.'

'Just come up on the chair and relax. Open wide. Oh dear . . .! Mr Maximus, I don't think you have been cleaning your teeth very well lately.'

The dentist went round Maximus' mouth, prodding with a sharp instrument.

'OUCH!' yelled Maximus, as loudly as he could with his mouth full of dentist.

'That's the one,' said Mr Pullem. 'You're going to need a small filling.'

'Well, Maximus. How's the toothache now?' asked Paula the next day when they met in the church.

'Fine thanks – that is to say, I haven't got it. Mr Pullem stopped the toothache when he gave me a filling. Do you want to see it?' asked Maximus pulling his mouth wide open with his front paw.

'No, thank you!' replied Paula. 'Tell me, Maximus, what exactly did Mr Pullem say to you?'

'He said that I must clean my teeth every day, that I must not eat too many sweet things because they are bad for my teeth, and that I must go to the dentist every six months.'

'I shall remind you about that,' said Paula. 'It's actually Peter's, Peregrine's, Pomegranite's and Petronella's birthday six months from now. That will remind me to remind you to go to the dentist. It makes sense you know. You must be responsible for your health – imagine what it would be like trying to eat hymnburgers without any teeth.'

Heavenly Father,
You have given us wonderful bodies. Help us to
understand that we must look after them. Thank you
for all those people who care for others – doctors,
nurses, dentists and so many more. Thank you for
good health. Amen.

Happy Christmas

It was Christmas Eve and Maximus was not happy. His front paws were stuck together with sticky tape and a ball of string had wound its way around his back paws and tail. In fact he was rolling around the floor of the vestry trying hard to get free when his friend Patrick came in.

'Oh, sorry Maximus, I can see you're a bit tied up at the moment! I'll come back later,' said Patrick, trying hard not to laugh.

'Christmas!' growled Maximus. 'Why does it always come too soon?'

'Er . . . I don't like to mention it, Maximus, but it usually is on December 25th. You have known about it for some time.'

'Oh, all right. I'm just not very good at Christmassing. It always seems to be such a rush. What am I going to give Paula? She's your wife, you should know what she wants.'

'Maximus, I know she would like a new saucepan. She burnt the last one cooking sermon note curry. But that's not what I've come for. I've come to invite you to

Christmas lunch tomorrow. The children want to show you their Nativity Play. Do come, please.'

'If I ever get untangled I would love to come. Thank you for the invitation.'

Patrick helped Maximus to get unstuck and unwound and left him in a pile of paper and cards. Maximus dashed out to the shops and just managed to buy a saucepan for Paula before they closed.

The next morning Maximus was woken by the joyful sound of the church bells wishing the whole world a happy Christmas. He stretched, groaned and yawned.

'What a noise! Can't they let you sleep on Christmas Day?' he moaned. 'Trust the church to spoil Christmas.'

He covered his ears with his paws, but it was no good, he could still hear the bells. He slowly got up, washed and shaved, and then started to get the presents ready for Patrick and Paula. The saucepan wasn't very well wrapped but he put it with the book he had bought for Patrick, called *Great Cheeses of the World*.

Just as the last people left the church after the morning service, Maximus picked up the parcels and went over to the Sunday School cupboard where Patrick and his family lived. At the last count there were at least sixty-three children. Mice always have large families, and Maximus had bought a large box of Chocolate Mouseteasers, hoping there would be enough for one each.

The smell drifting through the crack in the cupboard door was delicious. Maximus thought for a moment and then wiggled his whiskers – 'Um . . . I'm sure that's Carol Sheet Crumble with Holly Berry Sauce,' he said to himself. At that moment the door opened and Maximus was pulled and pushed in by dozens of tiny paws, all shouting 'Happy Christmas, Uncle Maximus,' at the tops of their shrill voices.

The lunch was very good indeed for Paula was a great cook. The children were well behaved and Patrick was very pleased with his book and Paula with her saucepan. In return they gave Maximus a new Crash Nut for when he went skate-boarding. Just as Maximus was feeling a doze coming over him he was led from the table to a comfy chair. All the mouslings had disappeared and only Patrick and Paula were left sitting next to Maximus.

As if from a long way away Maximus could hear his favourite carol, 'Once in Royal David's City', being sung. A choir of baby mice walked in slowly, singing the carol. They formed a horseshoe shape. When the carol had finished two of the children came in dressed as Mary and Joseph. Mary was sitting on the back of one of the larger children. They walked round the horseshoe and then Joseph stopped and, like the Bible story, knocked on the cupboard wall as if it were the door of the inn. A mouse wearing an apron came along and shook his head but pointed with his front paw to a pile of straw which Maximus could see in the corner. 'He means the stable where Jesus was born,' said Maximus to himself. And sure enough the children playing Mary and Joseph went into the straw and as the choir sang 'Away in a manger', Mary put the youngest baby mouse in a little manger.

The choir sang again – this time it was 'While shepherds watched their flocks by night'. On the other side of the cupboard Maximus could see several young mice dressed as shepherds and another group all in white.

'We did have a job choosing the angels!' whispered Paula to Maximus. As the carol ended, the shepherds went over to Mary and Joseph and the baby Jesus. When the shepherds left the little family, two of the older children came to the front of the horseshoe and spoke.

'Christmas is not about sticky tape and who I should send cards to. Christmas is about God loving the world so much that his son Jesus was born. Jesus is God's

own dear son and he was born in Bethlehem so that everyone could come to know and love God.'

The choir and the older mice sang 'O Come All Ye Faithful' and Maximus was very quiet and thoughtful after he had clapped the children.

Loving Father,
Thank you for Christmas – for the joy and fun, for the birth of Jesus, for the giving and receiving. Help us to receive your love in Jesus this Christmas. Amen.

Why be bored?

'I'm bored ... B.O.R.D ... bored!' said Maximus, whose spelling wasn't too good. 'Here I am, a healthy mouse with nothing to do. Everyone else has gone out, I've finished my library book, there's only old films on TV. I AM BORED!'

The empty church did not reply. Maximus's little squeak went round its walls and came back to him as a tiny echo ... 'bored, bored, bored'. He strode up and down the aisles, kicked at a cough sweet dropped by a choir boy, and stopped at last by the Notice Board.

'Even the notices are bored,' said Maximus to the church. 'It says so – Notice Board.' He climbed up and began to read the various pieces of paper. At the next meeting of the Young Wives Group there would be a speaker from the Gas Board. 'See, even the gas is bored,' muttered Maximus. The Sunday School needed another teacher, the church garden needed mowing and there was a list for people to put their names down to help, the Youth Group were going away for the weekend and there was a small notice asking for visitors to The Chestnuts, a Home for Old People.

'Nothing there to stop me being bored,' said Maximus. 'You would think the church would be able to find me something to do.' He went slowly back to the vestry and made himself a mug of Maxwell Mouse coffee. As he sipped the drink he began to think about that last little notice – the one about the old people. 'If I'm bored and can run about and go shopping and play games and read, it must be really boring if you're old and can't do those things.' He suddenly remembered the Home for Elderly Rodents where his uncle had lived until he died. It was called The Mouse Keeper. 'I wonder if they need any help?' Maximus asked himself.

Maximus walked up the drive towards the large house. The sun was shining brightly and the garden looked very beautiful with colourful flower beds, a large goldfish pond, and several old trees, now grown to a great height. He rang the door bell and asked to speak to the mouse in charge. He was taken to the office where he met Miss Cellany, the Manager.

'Mr Maximus, it is very good to see you. We remember your uncle well and we all miss his sense of fun. He often used to make us laugh with his stories.'

'I was wondering if you ever needed any help? There must be a lot to do looking after all these elderly mice. I could push a wheelchair or just sit and listen, if you wanted?'

'We would be very grateful,' said Miss Cellany. 'Our Care Assistants work very hard and don't always have time to stop and chat. Let me take you on a tour of the Home.'

They left the office and walked down a long corridor. There were some beautiful pictures on the walls between a number of doors.

'Every resident has their own room here at The Mouse Keeper,' said Miss Cellany. 'They bring in some of their favourite things from home – a chair, pictures and perhaps a chest of drawers. But you will remember that from when your uncle was here.'

'He was very happy,' said Maximus. 'He used to say that everyone was very kind and he certainly made lots of friends.'

'We try hard to make it as homely as possible,' said the Manager. 'It isn't easy when you're old, living close to other mice, especially when you have been used to your own home.'

They turned the corner at the end of the corridor and in front of them was a large lounge. Maximus could see lots of really comfortable chairs occupied by a number of grey haired older mice. There was some music and the mice were waving their paws about in time to it.

'Right,' said the Manager, 'now let's go back to the office and see when you can visit us. Some of our resident rodents don't see very well and love to have a book or the paper read to them. Others just like a bit of a chat. I know how much they will look forward to you coming.'

It was Wednesday – the day Maximus had arranged to go to The Mouse Keeper. He had worried about it during the night. What if they can't hear me? What if they don't like me? What if I don't know what to say? He dressed carefully, combed his whiskers, polished his shoes until they shone, and set off for the Home for Elderly Rodents.

When Maximus arrived he was introduced to an old grey haired mouse called Arthur Moe. Mr Moe was sitting in his room near the fire and looked as though he was almost asleep.

'Hello, young chap,' said the old mouse, much to Maximus' surprise. 'It's good to see you. I wonder if you would mind reading the paper for me. You see, I can't manage it now – all the words look a bit blurred.'

'Yes, no trouble at all,' replied Maximus and started

to read the Rodents' Gazette.

'The Prime Mouse announced in the Mouse of Commons that all pensions will be increased and there will be an extra ration of free cheese this coming Christmas. Loud squeaks greeted this from the Members of Parliament.'

After reading for a short time Maximus and the old gentlemouse had a long discussion about the world. Maximus found Mr Moe really interesting to chat to and the time passed very quickly.

'I can't understand,' said the elderly mouse, 'why it is today that so many young mice say they are bored. There was always something to do in my young days. Perhaps it's all this television? Do you get bored, Maximus?'

'Er . . . not now, Mr Moe. Not any longer,' replied Maximus.

Heavenly Father,
There are times when life seems boring, both at school and at home. Help us to use our time properly. Show us that there are others with whom we might spend our time to their benefit and our enjoyment. Amen.

Saints alight

The sun had got out of bed in a very good mood. It had decided to shine all day without a break. There was not a cloud in the sky and the wind had gone on holiday as well. It was a perfect day, warm and bright and cheerful.

A small mouse was wandering about St Michael's Church looking hopefully for something to eat. The mouse stopped, sat down, and scratched his head. There was something odd, something different, about the colour of the floor. Normally it was grey, with darker lines where the large stones met. Now it was . . . well, it was red and blue and green and brown and yellow and black and some more.

Maximus, who was the mouse sitting in the pool of colour, just couldn't understand it at all. Someone had been in the church, when he wasn't looking, painting the floor all these different shades. How dare they? What would everyone think? He tried scratching the colours with his front claws but it made no difference at all. He got a small bucket of water and a cloth and scrubbed as hard as he could but it still would not come off.

'Perhaps it's one of Patrick and Paula's children?' he

muttered to the empty church. 'Mouslings!' he went on. 'They just don't care today. No respect for anyone or anything. It's what they call giraffeety – that's what it is.'

Maximus scampered up the church and stopped, panting, outside the Sunday School cupboard where Patrick and the family lived. He knocked as hard as he could on the door.

'Hullo, Maximus,' said Patrick yawning. 'Sorry, but we overslept this morning. Is there anything you want?'

'I want to know who done it!' said Maximus shouting. 'One of your juvenile detergents has painted the church floor – not just one colour but lots. It's a disgrace!'

'Hold on, Maximus. You'll burst a button off your shirt if you get so angry. Now tell me calmly, please, what's happened.'

'Parents should be responsible for their children. That's what I say.'

'Maximus, I don't know what you are talking about.'

'There!' pointed Maximus. 'Just down there – in the island. There's lots of paint on the floor.'

'I think you mean aisle,' said Patrick. 'All right, I'll come and look.'

The two mice walked down the aisle of the church until they came to the colours on the floor.

'That's funny,' said Maximus. 'It's moved a little bit. It was nearer the pillar before,' he said. 'Are you sure some of your children aren't playing games in the church?'

'They're all at home,' said Patrick. 'Not one of them is out. It must be someone else. Come and have some Maxwell Mouse coffee and then we'll go and ask Barnabas if he has seen anything.'

Barnabas is the church bat who lives in the belfry, which he calls the battery. He is a very wise bat who normally sleeps during the day and wakes up at night. In the summer he eats crickets and grasshoppers, which is why he is sometimes called the Cricket Bat.

Maximus and Patrick climbed the stairs into the belfry, with difficulty. They were too out of breath to speak until they reached the top.

'Er . . . excuse us, please, Barnabas,' said Maximus. 'We have a problem.'

'It is only when some problematical event occurs that you present yourselves in my campanile. I imagine that it is your anticipation that I shall be able to solve the current conundrum?'

'Er . . . yes, I think so,' said a rather confused Maximus. 'You see we have a secret floor painter in the church who comes and paints colours and then they move and then after a bit they move again and Patrick says it isn't any of his.'

'Your presentation of the predicament is such that I have less than a totally clear comprehension of the issue you are posing. However, it is my experience that your saintly named companion is generally better equipped to offer a satisfactory explanation.'

'He means you, Patrick,' whispered Maximus.

Ten minutes later two mice and one bat could be seen looking closely at the colours on the aisle floor. The patch of colour had moved again during their visit to the belfry.

'Saints alight!' exclaimed Barnabas.

'Pardon?' said Maximus and Patrick as one.

'The juxtaposition of the solar orb in conjunction with the multi-coloured fenestration has projected the colours contained in the stained glass window.'

'Pardon?' said Maximus, repeating himself.

'I think what he means is that the sun is shining through the stained glass window. You know, the window with St Peter and St Paul in it,' said Patrick. Both mice turned and looked. Sure enough the bright sunlight was shining through the large window with the picture of the two saints. Because the angle of the sun changed through the day, so the colours moved slowly round the church floor.

'I see comprehension has dawned,' said Barnabas, and he flew back to the belfry.

'I often wondered what saints were for,' said Maximus. 'Now I know. They let in the light and add bright colours where places are dull.'

'You don't have to live in a stained glass window to do that,' said Patrick. 'There's lots of people, and mice, who make dark things better.'

'I think that's what Jesus does,' said Maximus. 'If you look in the other window there is a picture of Jesus. The words underneath say, "I am the light of the world. Whoever follows me will have the light of life and never walk in darkness." '

Heavenly Father,
Thank you for all those who make dark days brighter.
Help us to follow Jesus, who came to bring light into
a dark world, and then to reflect his light to others.
Amen.

A load of rubbish

'Help! Help me, please!'

'Where? Where are you?' answered Maximus, as he searched anxiously in the graveyard of St Michael's Church.

'Over here,' came the answer. 'Just near the gate, by the rubbish tip.'

Maximus had been outside, enjoying the sunshine and taking a short stroll before tea, when he heard the cry for help. He scampered off towards the churchyard gate, past his little garden, and saw something move in the long grass. The something shouted again.

'Oh, help me please! I'm just here. I can't move at all. Please help.'

Maximus ran into the grass. There in front of him was a very small and very frightened hedgehoglet. It was Hyacinth, the daughter of Henrietta. The baby hedgehog was trapped by one hind paw. She was stuck in an empty fizzy drink can which was half buried in the ground. Maximus crawled down to the little hedgehog and spoke gently to her.

'It's all right,' he said. 'You'll be free in just a moment.

40

You must just help me by being brave.'

He lifted her paw slowly until it was clear of the can. He looked at it carefully.

'You've been very brave,' he said. 'I don't think there's any damage done but you'd better get your mum to look at it. I'll come home with you so you don't fall into anything else on the way.'

The two animals walked slowly through the graveyard until Hyacinth spotted her mother.

'Where have you been?' asked Henrietta.

'I fell into an empty can and I was ever so frightened and I didn't know what to do and I shouted and shouted and Uncle Maximus came along and he pulled me out and my leg hurts a bit and what's for tea?'

Maximus laughed and was soon joined by Henrietta.

'I don't think there is too much wrong with you,' said her mother, 'if you want to know what's for tea! The answer is earthworm spaghetti. However, it seems to me that it's more important to thank Uncle Maximus very much for rescuing you.'

'So that's what happened,' said Maximus to the group of animals sitting in front of him. 'And it is all because of the litter.'

'Excuse me, Maximus, but my litter's got nothing to do with it,' said Roberta the rabbit. 'My children are good children.'

'I mean rubbish when I say litter,' said Maximus.

'Say what you mean then,' said Roberta.

'What,' said Patrick, trying hard to change the subject, 'shall we do about it?'

'I suggest that we have a complication,' said Maximus. 'The team which picks up most lit . . . er, rubbish, is the winner.'

'Maximus is right,' said Patrick. 'We should have a competition – not complication, Maximus.'

'I agree,' said Herbert. 'After all, Maximus, it was my

granddaughter that you rescued. We must do something to stop our children from being hurt. Humans just throw rubbish anywhere. They never think of the harm which it does to us animals.'

They all agreed that next day they would have a Rubbish Collecting Competition.

Before ten o'clock all the teams had gathered outside the church door waiting for the clock to strike. The Magic Mice were led by Maximus with Patrick, Paula and their mouslings, the Racing Rabbits by Robert and Roberta and their children. The Happy Hedgehogs included Herbert, Henrietta and Hyacinth and there was another team – the Brainy Bats, but since they would only come out at night, they were disqualified.

As the clock struck ten the teams ran off to different parts of the churchyard. The Racing Rabbits started by the gate and began picking up the cans that had been thrown over the churchyard wall. The Happy Hedgehogs looked very strange as they began to roll over and over in prickly balls. The others stopped laughing when they saw how much paper and plastic stuck to the prickles. The Magic Mice formed a circle with the mouslings round the edge and the grown ups inside. There had been a wedding on the previous Saturday. Every mousling picked up a piece of confetti and it was handed into the middle of the circle where Maximus kept a paw on it to stop it blowing away.

The morning went on and soon the rabbits had collected all the cans, some with very sharp edges. The hedgehogs had found all the larger pieces of paper and the mice the smaller ones. The piles got higher and higher. One of the baby rabbits cut his paw on some glass from a broken bottle and needed a bandage, and one of the hedgehogs was nearly suffocated in a large supermarket plastic bag.

The clock struck twelve and all the animals came

together. The rabbits' pile, with all the cans, was the largest.

'All the teams have done very well,' said Robert. 'We don't think there needs to be a prize because we have only done what everyone should do all the time – that is tidy up. I wish that humans would take a lesson from us. They drop rubbish and animals get hurt.'

They took all the rubbish they had collected to the dustbin in the churchyard. The human animals were quite surprised to see how tidy it was when they came to church but they never knew how it had happened.

Heavenly Father,
You have a beautiful world for us to live in but we often spoil it. We drop rubbish, we pollute water, we waste what you have given us. Forgive us for our selfishness and help us to look after your world properly so that all may enjoy it. Amen.

You are who you are

'Wait! Stop! Hold it!' shouted Patrick. 'MAXIMUS . . . WHAT ARE YOU DOING?'

Patrick had just come into the church from the Sunday School cupboard. As he looked around he saw Maximus, at least he thought it was Maximus. His friend was balanced on his back paws on the edge of the pulpit. Stuck to each front paw was a page from a hymn book, folded in the shape of a bird's wing.

As Patrick was about to shout again, Maximus yelled 'Geronimouse!' and launched himself into space. Patrick covered his eyes with his paws and waited for a crash. What he actually heard was more of a splash, followed by a . . .

'Help! Get me out of here! I'm drowning . . . glug, glug, glug.'

Patrick rushed round to the front of the pulpit and saw what had happened. Maximus had been very lucky. He had landed in a large vase of chrysanthemums, breaking both his fall and the flowers, and then sliding down them into the water. His paper wings were soaking up the water and getting in the way of his attempts to

climb out.

After a lot of effort, Patrick managed to disentangle Maximus from the flowers and the sodden hymn pages. He noticed that one of the hymns said something about 'for those in peril on the sea' but didn't like to tell Maximus.

'Thanks, Patrick,' said Maximus scratching his head and shaking the water from his fur. 'Something went wrong. I think it was the shape of the wings. I shall have to look at Barnabas more closely.'

'Maximus, what are you trying to do?'

'Couldn't you see? I thought it was obvious. I am going to fly. If bats can do it then so can any self respecting mouse. It's just a question of aerodynamite. Back to the drawing board.'

'But Maximus, bats are meant to fly – mice ARE NOT! You will end up hurting yourself. You could kill yourself. Please don't ever try again. Now go back into the vestry and put on some dry clothes. Be happy being a mouse.'

The two friends did not meet for several days. Patrick was just beginning to wonder if Maximus was all right when there was a loud banging on the Sunday School cupboard door.

'Quick! Come quickly, please,' begged a baby rabbit, whom Patrick recognised as Robin. 'It's Maximus. He's got himself stuck underground.'

Patrick dashed out of the church and there, near to the church gate, was a crowd of very worried looking rabbits and hedgehogs. They were standing around a small and rather deep looking hole. When they saw Patrick they all started to talk at once.

'Maximus is down . . .'

'He's stuck and he can't . . .'

'He borrowed my best spade and then . . .'

'Don't know how we can get him . . .'

'Please, everybody,' asked Patrick. 'One of you tell

47

me what's happened.'

'Well,' said Robert, 'Maximus came early this morning and borrowed my spade. He said something about "if rabbits can live in burrows then so can mice." He wouldn't listen to me when I told him rabbits is rabbits and mice is mice.'

'Right,' said Patrick. 'Quiet everyone. Let's see if we can hear anything.' He put his ear to the top of the hole. All the hedgehogs and mice were quite still. After a short time Patrick could just about hear a very faint noise. It sounded like 'Get me out. I'm stu . . . ck.'

'Now listen to me,' said Patrick, climbing to the top of the small pile of earth dug from the hole. 'Herbert, organise your hedgehogs to start digging over there at an angle. Robert, do the same with your family but start over here. One of the two tunnels should reach Maximus. We can't go in behind him or the earth will cover him up.'

The two teams started digging furiously. Soon there were two piles of earth and stones and roots on either side of Maximus' hole. Both teams changed diggers every few minutes. Patrick kept calling down the first hole to tell Maximus to stay calm. Time went on and it began to get dark. Paula and some of her family scampered into the church and came out with some candles.

It was Horatio, Herbert Hedgehog's son-in-law, who was the first to reach the little mouse. He was deep in the tunnel, pushing the soil away, when he heard a faint squeak. He scraped more earth away and Maximus tumbled into Horatio's tunnel. At the same time another tunnel opened and Richard, Robert's oldest son, appeared. With Richard pushing and Horatio dragging they soon had Maximus out of the tunnel and into the open. Paula rushed over and gave him a drink.

'I was only trying to be like a rabbit,' said Maximus to Patrick the next day. 'I thought that if rabbits could live in burrows then mice might try it. It would be less draughty than the church.'

'Maximus, you've tried flying like a bat. You've tried digging like a rabbit. Why can't you realise that you are a mouse? Mice don't fly. Mice do not dig tunnels. Mice do mousy things. When they try to do other things they hurt themselves and make a lot of trouble for other animals who have to rescue them.'

'Yes, I know you're right. But sometimes I wish I was somebody else,' said Maximus. 'I did think I might see what being a water rat was like . . .'

'DON'T YOU DARE!' warned Patrick.

Heavenly Father,
You have made us as we are. Help us to make the best of ourselves without worrying about being different. Help us to work and play as well as we can so that we enjoy being ourselves. Amen.

What a wonderful world

'I'm not sure that I want to,' said Maximus.

'Oh, go on. I promise you'll enjoy it if you only make the effort,' said Paula.

'Yes, but two hours on a coach seems an awful long time.'

'But it stops for a break on the way and there's lots to see out of the windows,' encouraged Paula.

'Oh, all right, I'll come. You won't give up until I agree.'

Patrick and Paula had been trying to persuade Maximus to come out for the day on a coach trip. Herbert and his family had promised to look after all the mouselings so Patrick, Paula and Maximus could go out by themselves without the children. Maximus wasn't very keen to go.

Next morning at eight o'clock Patrick and Paula were waiting anxiously outside the church. They kept looking first at the church clock and then at the vestry door.

'It'll be here soon,' said Paula. 'I knew he wouldn't come.'

'I think he will,' said her husband. 'It's just that he doesn't like getting up.'

At that moment they heard the sound of the coach coming up the road. It drew up outside the church gate. Just as they were climbing the steps a strange looking figure came hurtling out of the church yard. It was wearing a pair of blue jeans but it appeared that there was a nightshirt tail hanging out at the back. Its fur wasn't combed and it was struggling into a T shirt.

'Sorry, but I got stuck in my bed,' said Maximus.

'You mean you couldn't get out of it!' said Patrick.

'Well, something like that. Now where are we going?'

'To Northend-on-Sea. It has the shortest pier in the world. It's famous for its rock,' replied Paula.

'We drive through some beautiful countryside on the way,' said Patrick, 'so no falling asleep.'

They went out of the town and the road was soon leading through open fields. In the distance were green hills with little dots of white scattered all over them. As they got nearer they could see the dots turn into sheep. They crossed a river bordered by old willow trees and just caught a glimpse of a kingfisher, its brilliant colours shining in the sun. Maximus was turning from side to side, looking first out of one window and then another. He got quite excited telling Patrick and Paula all he could see, forgetting they could see it too.

'Quick, look,' he said. 'Did you see that old thatched cottage? Bet some lucky mouse lives there! Look at that field of poppies. Look at those ducks on that pond. Look at that old bridge – bet that's been there a long time.'

Maximus even seemed quite disappointed when they stopped at a café for a cup of Maxwell Mouse coffee. Soon they were back in the coach again and began to smell the sea. As they got nearer to Northend they could see the masts of the ships in the harbour. The coach stopped on the sea front and they all got out. The driver reminded them to be back again at four o'clock or the coach would go without them.

The three mice walked along the promenade looking at the waves and the circling seagulls. They bought ice-creams and paid for three deck chairs which they put up on the sand, not far from the edge of the tide. Maximus put on his Macho Mouse swimming trunks and, together with the other two, went dashing into the sea. They all had a great swim and came out feeling very hungry. After a quick rub down with their towels they tucked into the ant flavoured crisps and cheese and candle sandwiches that Paula had packed.

'Oh dear,' yawned Maximus, 'I'm feeling like a little doze. It's been a busy morning.'

Patrick and Paula agreed and they were all soon fast asleep. As they slept the waves grew higher and higher until after half an hour or so they were washing the feet of the little deck chairs. Moments later the first deck chair rocked gently and then began to float. It was followed by the other two. It was Maximus who woke first.

'Patrick! Paula!' he shouted. 'Wake up – we're all at sea. Call the Air Mouse Rescue. Do something!'

The sea was slowly washing the three deck chairs further away from the shore. The three mice were drifting apart and the waves were getting higher so that their little deck chair boats were being tossed up and down. They could only see each other when they were on top of a wave.

Fortunately for the three, a seagull swooped low over the waves and realised what was happening. He screeched for two friends, who left the pieces of fish they were eating, and flew over the mice. The three birds dived down together and each plucked a mouse up in their beaks. They flew to the shore and dropped them gently on to the edge of the promenade.

'Dangerous thing the sea,' said the leader. 'You have to be careful or it can spoil your day.'

'Thank you so much,' said Patrick. 'You really saved our lives after we had been very silly.'

'Yes, thank you very much,' said both Maximus and Paula.

'We shall have to scamper to catch the coach,' said Patrick. They got to it just as the driver was thinking it was time to go without them.

All the way back to St Michael's Church they talked about the day.

'I've really enjoyed it,' said Maximus. 'It was a lovely drive. The country is so beautiful.'

'I agree,' said Paula. 'It's been a really good day. Nice to be out without the children, but I am looking forward to seeing them again. I do hope that Herbert has been all right.'

'We have had a great day,' said Patrick, 'but we nearly spoilt it by doing something really silly. The Air Mouse Rescue team were brilliant, weren't they? They are very brave.'

Heavenly Father,
Thank you for the beautiful world you have given us to enjoy. Help us to treat it with respect so that we do not put others in danger by our carelessness. Thank you for the courage of all those who work for the rescue services. Amen.

When in doubt, read the instructions

One moment it was there and the next moment it had gone. Maximus sat for a few seconds in total darkness, hoping it would come back. He hoped some kind voice would say, 'We are very sorry about the loss of picture but it is due to a fault at the transmitter.' But nothing happened. He had been in the middle of one of his favourite television programmes 'Mouse Party', in which famous mice were interviewed and then they chose a piece of music. Willy, of Willy and the Whisker Bangers, had just chosen Gerry and the Gerbils singing their current hit, when the television went dead.

Maximus quickly lit a candle and made sure that the plug hadn't fallen out of the socket on the wall. He tapped the set with his front paws but that made no difference at all. He decided that there was nothing for it but to get help. He scampered off to the Sunday School cupboard where he found Patrick and Paula, surrounded by thirty-seven of their children, still watching 'Mouse Party'.

'Come in, Maximus,' said Patrick, 'just watching the last few moments. Won't be a moment. I thought this

was one of your favourite programmes?'

'It is,' replied Maximus, 'it's just a bit difficult to see on a blank screen.'

They watched the end of the programme and Paula sent the mouslings off to bed each with a cup of Morelicks.

'What's the problem?' asked Patrick.

'My set's upset,' said Maximus. 'It's ill. It won't work. I missed the best bit of 'Mouse Party' 'cos it went black.'

'Sounds serious,' said Patrick. 'I'll come and have a look. Shan't be long, dear,' he said to Paula.

The two mice ran back to the vestry and re-lit the candle. Patrick unplugged the set from the wall and unscrewed the back. As he did so his whiskers twitched and he sneezed very loudly.

'When did you dust this last?' he asked, sneezing again.

'I think it was this year,' said Maximus laughing. 'Might not have been.'

'Well, I can't see anything wrong,' said Patrick, after a few moments, during which time he sneezed again twice. 'Television is really clever, isn't it? There's mice all over the world and we can see them. Do you remember those brill pictures on the Mouse Moon Landing? "One small scamper for mouse, one large scamper for mousekind." Just amazing that we could see it all happen down here!'

'But what am I going to do?' asked Maximus. 'It'll be Coronation Mouseholes tomorrow night. I can't miss that.'

'I think we may have to ask Barnabas in the morning,' replied his friend. 'He's clever. He'll know what to do. Now I'm off to bed.'

The two mice climbed the belfry steps soon after breakfast and found Barnabas, the church bat, just settling down to sleep after his night's work looking after the church.

57

'Oh no!' said Barnabas rather rudely. 'It's Minibus and Peastick, the revolting rodents. I anticipate a problem needing my superior cranium.'

'Please, Mr Barnabas, we're really sorry to bother you but we need your advice. You see Maximus's telly isn't working. It's gone black,' said Patrick.

'And I can't hear anything either,' said Maximus.

'Is it essential that you disturb my nocturnal aspirations on a Sunday morning simply because your wretched electronic device has failed?' asked Barnabas. 'We bats have used electronic devices for millions of years. We are undoubtedly the most advanced of all creatures. Have you considered consulting the manufacturer's almanac? Their Instruction Manuals often provide the solutions to these technical enigmas.'

'That's it,' said Patrick. 'That's what we should have done, Maximus. Looked at the book that came with the set.'

The two mice went back down the steep belfry steps after thanking Barnabas. They searched the vestry and after a short time found a scruffy looking book with the title *Rodent Rentals Television Set – Mark Five*.

'That's the one, look in there,' said Maximus, who wasn't the best reader of the two. 'What does it say?'

'Page six – Faults,' said Patrick turning the pages. 'Ah, here we are. "If the set goes blank then there are three possible ways of repairing it.

1. Make sure the power is getting to the set.

2. Make sure all switches are turned on.

3. Check no wires have become loose inside the set. Before you do this unplug the set from the power supply."

It must be a loose wire,' said Patrick. 'We've checked all the other things. Hand me the screwdriver, please.'

Patrick almost disappeared into the back of the television set and soon started sneezing again. After a few moments Maximus heard a rather muffled shout.

'I've found it. Should be all right again now.' And Patrick backed out of the television, covered in dust.

They screwed the back on, pushed the plug into the socket on the wall and turned it on. Almost at once they saw a picture of the inside of a church and heard a voice. It was the Sunday Service. The minister was speaking to the children.

'Sometimes,' he said, 'our special toys go wrong. Perhaps the computer won't work or the gears on your mountain bike won't change. What do we do then? It's usually a matter of asking your dad or mum to fix it. When all else fails, they read the Instruction Manual.

'Sometimes,' he went on, 'things go wrong in our lives. We do things we know are not right. We get cross and angry with other people or we get into trouble because we want something which isn't ours. Sometimes we don't seem to be able to make things better on our own. It's then we need the special Instruction Manual that God has given us. It's called the Bible. It's full of very good advice on how to live our lives so things don't go wrong AND what to do when they do. If you read some every day you'll find it makes a big difference.'

'Fancy that,' said Maximus. 'Humans have an Instruction Manual just like my telly. I hope they read it!'

Heavenly Father,
Thank you for the Bible, for all that we can read about you in it, and for all that it can teach us. Help us when we read it to understand what you are telling us and then do it. Amen.

Good for something

It was Tuesday evening, the evening that the church organist came to practise. Maximus always enjoyed hearing the organ being played and he crept out of the vestry and sat under the front pew to listen. He could see Johann Sebastian, the organist's cat, sitting on the organ stool and helping to turn the pages of the music. Sometimes Maximus joined in on his mouse organ. The organist was very good and loved playing the organ, even to what he thought was an empty church. He practised the hymns for next Sunday and the music he would play before and after the services. Maximus just sat and felt the music fill the church.

'It was really brilliant last night,' Maximus said to Patrick the next morning. 'He is so clever making wonderful music like that. I wish I was good at something.'

'Everybody has different gifts,' said Patrick. 'Barnabas is brainy, Robert the rabbit is a very good gardener, Herbert can see at night.'

'That's all very well,' replied Maximus, 'but I can't think of anything I can do. I can't play the organ or paint pictures or write books. I'm not even very good at

skate boarding – I keep falling off.'

'I'm sure there are things that you are good at. Now, come on, you promised me a game of football.'

The two mice went out of the church and on to the car park where the vicar and the organist parked their cars. They had found an old table tennis ball, thrown away by the Youth Club, and started to pass it to each other. Several of Patrick's sons came and joined them and before long Maximus began to realise he must be getting old. He was soon out of breath chasing the young mice.

'Can't even run as fast I used to,' he panted to Patrick. 'Young Peregrine and Percival are much quicker than me.'

After another ten minutes or so Maximus wandered slowly back to the vestry and lay down on his duvet. He was soon fast asleep.

Outside in the churchyard, Patrick was visiting several friends. First he went to find Herbert the hedgehog.

'So that's all right then. You'll be there. That's it – Monday 26th June.'

The hedgehog agreed and went off to tell the rest of the family.

Nearer to the churchyard gate was the home burrow of Robert and the rabbits. Patrick caught Robert just as he was coming out.

'Yes. That's fine. I'll be there and bring all the family – well, most of them,' said Robert.

As the sun began to sink and tuck itself up in a fluffy woollen cloud for the night, Barnabas flew silently down from the belfry looking for midges to eat.

'Totally in agreement, Peastick,' said the bat. 'Oh most definitely, count me amongst those present on the day.'

Patrick's next visit was the most dangerous. Later that evening he set off out of the church towards the big oak tree which grew in one corner of the churchyard. The tree was the home of Mr Toot, the tawny owl. He knew that Mr Toot enjoyed mice pudding so he had to be very careful. Patrick had written out a message for the owl which he left spread out on the ground under the tree. He hoped the bird would see it.

'That only leaves Johann Sebastian,' said Patrick to Paula the next morning. 'I shall see him later but I'm sure he will want to be there.'

As the days grew closer to the twenty-sixth Maximus found it hard to understand why it was that his old friend Patrick just didn't seem to be about very much. When he went round to the Sunday School cupboard Patrick was always out.

Maximus woke up on the morning of Monday the twenty-sixth and stretched himself. He yawned once or twice and then slowly got out of bed and got dressed. There was something puzzling him. Something he should remember but couldn't. Something important. Whatever was it? He was still scratching his head when he wandered out into the church. He nearly bumped into Patrick who was carrying an enormous supermarket bag.

'Sorry, Maximus, er . . . can't stop now,' said his friend. 'Just been doing the shopping for the family. By the way, do hope you can come to supper tonight. See you about eight o'clock.'

'Thanks,' said Maximus. 'I shall look forward to that.'

At eight o'clock, just as Maximus had finished getting dressed, there was a knock on the vestry door. In came Patrick and Paula with thirty seven mouselings. They were followed by Robert and Roberta with lots of baby rabbits. Herbert Hedgehog and Henrietta his daughter, together with Hyacinth, his granddaughter, came next. Barnabas flew in followed by Mr. Toot and, last of all, Johann Sebastian.

Patrick counted 'One, Two, Three.' They all began to sing.

> *Happy birthday to you,*
> *Happy birthday to you,*
> *Happy birthday, dear Maximus,*
> *Happy birthday to you.*

Patrick stood up in front of the whole crowd. He put his paw to his lips and everyone went quiet.

'Maximus, today is a very special day, your birthday. We have come because we want to thank you for being a very special mouse. A few days ago you told me that there wasn't anything you could do. You couldn't play the organ, or garden or be brainy. Your friends here think otherwise.'

'I want to thank you,' said Herbert, 'for rescuing my granddaughter Hyacinth, when she cut her paw.'

'And I want to thank you for giving us all the food from the Harvest Festival when we were starving,' said Robert.

'And I know, Minibus, that no one looks after the church better than you do – during the day that is,' said Barnabas.

'I've always enjoyed being Tom to your Jerry,' said Johann Sebastian.

'And I know that it was you who helped my baby Tootsie when she tried to fly too soon,' said Mr Toot.

'And most of all,' said Paula, 'we all know that it was you, Maximus, who found us a new home in the church.'

'You see,' said Patrick, 'there are lots of things that you can do and have done. You're a very special mouse, Maximus. Thank you.'

And they all had a wonderful party.

Heavenly Father,
Sometimes we become jealous of what other people can do and forget what gifts you have given us. Help us to discover your gifts and to use them wisely for your sake and for ours. Amen.